Did You See Chip?

Did You See Chip?

Wong Herbert Yee
Illustrated by Laura Ovresat

Green Light Readers
Harcourt, Inc.
Orlando Austin New York San Diego Toronto London

Kim

Dad

Chip

Mr. Sanchez

Hot Dog Man

Park Worker

"I miss our farm," said Kim. "I wish we
had friends here in the city."
"Sometimes it's hard to be in a new
house," said Dad.

"Let's take Chip for a walk," said
Dad. "That will help cheer us up."
"Yip-yip! Yip-yip!" said Chip.

"Stop, Chip! Come back!" said Kim.
"We need to catch him," said Dad.
"He could get lost in this big city.
Let's go!"

"Hi!" said Kim. "Did you see my dog, Chip?"
"Is he a little black dog with a yip-yip bark?"
asked Mr. Sanchez.
"That's our Chip!" said Kim.

"I think he ran to the park. I'll help you catch him," said Mr. Sanchez.

"Hi!" said Kim. "Did you see my dog, Chip?"
"Is he a little black dog with a yip-yip bark?"
asked the Hot Dog Man.
"That's our Chip!" said Kim.

"I think he ran to the swings. I'll help you catch him," said the Hot Dog Man.

"Hi!" said Kim. "Did you see my dog, Chip?"
"Is he a little black dog with a yip-yip bark?"
asked the Park Worker.
"That's our Chip!" said Kim.

"I think he ran out of the park. I'll help you catch him," said the Park Worker.

"Look!" said Mr. Sanchez.
"There on the steps!" said the Hot Dog Man.
"It's the little black dog with the yip-yip bark!" said the Park Worker.

"Chip!" said Kim.
"What a smart dog!" said Dad. "He came home. He didn't get lost at all."

"Thanks for helping us catch Chip,"
said Kim.

"Kim, it looks as if you got your wish," said Dad.

"Yes," said Kim. "Now we have some
new friends in the city."
"Yip-yip! Yip-yip!" said Chip.

Think About It

1. Why do Kim and Dad run out of their house?

2. How do Kim, Dad, and Chip make new friends?

3. Do you think Kim will like the city more from now on? Why or why not?

4. Have you ever moved to a new place? Tell a friend about your move.

Make a Friend

It's fun to make a new friend!

WHAT YOU'LL NEED

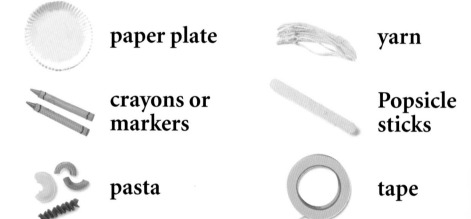

paper plate

yarn

crayons or markers

Popsicle sticks

pasta

tape

1 Make a paper plate puppet that looks like your new friend.

2 Have your friend make a puppet that looks like you.

3 When you're done, tape a Popsicle stick to the back of each puppet.

Then you can:

- Let your puppets do the talking.
  Use the puppets to tell stories about
  you and your new friend.

- Have a puppet show.
  Act out a way to be a good friend.

Meet the Author and Illustrator

At first, Wong Herbert Yee only illustrated children's books. Then he decided it would be interesting to write the stories, too. He hopes that you will have fun reading *Did You See Chip?*

Wong Herbert Yee

Laura Ovresat loves to draw. She also loves dogs. When she drew the pictures for this book, she thought about the dog she had when she was little. Even when she was having a bad day, that dog made her feel good—just like Chip!

Laura Ovresat

www.HarcourtBooks.com

First Green Light Readers edition 2004
Green Light Readers is a trademark of Harcourt, Inc., registered in the
United States of America and/or other jurisdictions.

Library of Congress Cataloging-in-Publication Data
Yee, Wong Herbert.
Did you see Chip?/Wong Herbert Yee; illustrated by Laura Ovresat.
p. cm.
"Green Light Readers."
Summary: After moving to the city, Kim makes some new friends
while looking for her lost dog, Chip.
[1. Dogs—Fiction. 2. Moving, Household—Fiction.
3. Lost and found possessions—Fiction. 4. Friendship—Fiction.
5. City and town life—Fiction.]
I. Ovresat, Laura, ill. II. Title. III. Series: Green Light Reader.
PZ7.Y3655Di 2004
[E]—dc22   2003012866
ISBN 0-15-205095-7
ISBN 0-15-205096-5 pb

A C E G H F D B
A C E G H F D B (pb)

Ages 5-7
Grades: 1-2
Guided Reading Level: I-J
Reading Recovery Level: 16

Green Light Readers
For the reader who's ready to GO!

"A must-have for any family with a beginning reader."—*Boston Sunday Herald*

"You can't go wrong with adding several copies of these terrific books to your beginning-to-read collection."—*School Library Journal*

"A winner for the beginner."—*Booklist*

Five Tips to Help Your Child Become a Great Reader

1. Get involved. Reading aloud to and with your child is just as important as encouraging your child to read independently.

2. Be curious. Ask questions about what your child is reading.

3. Make reading fun. Allow your child to pick books on subjects that interest her or him.

4. Words are everywhere—not just in books. Practice reading signs, packages, and cereal boxes with your child.

5. Set a good example. Make sure your child sees YOU reading.

Why Green Light Readers Is the Best Series for Your New Reader

● Created exclusively for beginning readers by some of the biggest and brightest names in children's books

● Reinforces the reading skills your child is learning in school

● Encourages children to read—and finish—books by themselves

● Offers extra enrichment through fun, age-appropriate activities unique to each story

● Incorporates characteristics of the Reading Recovery program used by educators

● Developed with Harcourt School Publishers and credentialed educational consultants

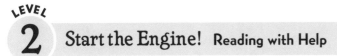

Daniel's Mystery Egg
Alma Flor Ada/G. Brian Karas

Animals on the Go
Jessica Brett/Richard Cowdrey

Marco's Run
Wesley Cartier/Reynold Ruffins

Digger Pig and the Turnip
Caron Lee Cohen/Christopher Denise

Tumbleweed Stew
Susan Stevens Crummel/Janet Stevens

The Chick That Wouldn't Hatch
Claire Daniel/Lisa Campbell Ernst

Splash!
Ariane Dewey/Jose Aruego

Get That Pest!
Erin Douglas/Wong Herbert Yee

Why the Frog Has Big Eyes
Betsy Franco/Joung Un Kim

I Wonder
Tana Hoban

A Bed Full of Cats
Holly Keller

The Fox and the Stork
Gerald McDermott

Try Your Best
Robert McKissack/Joe Cepeda

Boots for Beth
Alex Moran/Lisa Campbell Ernst

Catch Me If You Can!
Bernard Most

The Very Boastful Kangaroo
Bernard Most

Farmers Market
Carmen Parks/Edward Martinez

Shoe Town
Janet Stevens/Susan Stevens Crummel

The Enormous Turnip
Alexei Tolstoy/Scott Goto

Where Do Frogs Come From?
Alex Vern

The Purple Snerd
Rozanne Lanczak Williams/
Mary GrandPré

Did You See Chip?
Wong Herbert Yee/Laura Ovresat

Look for more Green Light Readers wherever books are sold!